For peace in stormy times.

First published in the United States
by Phyllis Fogelman Books
An imprint of Penguin Putnam Books for Young Readers
345 Hudson Street
New York, New York 10014

Published in Great Britain
by Frances Lincoln Limited
Text copyright © 2002 by Laurence Anholt
Illustrations copyright © 2002 by Catherine Anholt
All rights reserved
Printed in Hong Kong
1 3 5 7 9 10 8 6 4 2

Library of Congress Cataloging-in-Publication Data
Anholt, Catherine.
Chimp and Zee and the big storm / Catherine and Laurence Anholt.
p. cm.
Summary: Two little chimpanzees have an adventure when stormy winds lift them up from
their house in the coconut tree and carry them out over the sea.
ISBN 0-8037-2700-3
[1. Chimpanzees—Fiction. 2. Storms—Fiction.] I. Anholt, Laurence. II. Title.
PZ7.A58635 Ch 2002 [E]—dc21 2001050155

The illustrations were made using a combination of pencil,
ink, and watercolor. The images were then cut out
and pasted onto colored papers.

Come and meet Chimp and Zee at the Anholts' website — www.anholt.co.uk

Chimp and Zee
and the BIG STORM

Catherine and
Laurence Anholt

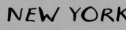

PHYLLIS FOGELMAN BOOKS ✒ NEW YORK

This is Chimp.   This is Zee.

It's a stormy day in the coconut tree.

The rain rattles on the roof.
The wind whistles around the windows.
It is too stormy to go out and play.
Chimp and Zee do not want
to do anything together.

They squibble and
squabble and drive
everyone bananas.
Until . . .
SNAP!

"Chimp did it."

"Zee did it."

"I wasn't even there."

"Zee did it."

"Chimp did it."

"It's just NOT FAIR!"

"Oh, you chumpy chimps," sighs Mumkey.

Papakey looks at the windy garden.
"Goodness!" he says. "We've left the wash outside.
I will fetch it, before it blows away."

Chimp and Zee want to go out too.
They are not afraid of the Big Storm.
"You must hold tight to Papakey," says Mumkey.
"And you must not squibble and squabble."

It is VERY windy outside.
Chimp and Zee do NOT hold tight to Papakey.

They DO squibble
and squabble.

They monkey around
and drive
Papakey bananas.

Then, **WHOOSH!**
A pair of Mumkey's pants blows right up into a tree.

"Chimp did it."

"Zee did it."

"I wasn't even there."

"Zee did it."

"Chimp did it."

"It's just NOT FAIR!"

"Oh, you chumpy chimps," sighs Papakey.

Then Chimp and Zee try to help. They fold a big sheet.

But suddenly there is another gust of wind. . . .

Whoo-OOSH!!

When Papakey turns around,
the sheet is flying
through the air like a kite . . .

and so are
Chimp and Zee!

Mumkey hears shouting.
She sees Chimp and Zee
float past the window.

"Come down!"
cry Mumkey and Papakey.
"Little monkeys
should not fly."

"Wa! Wa! WAA!" shouts Chimp.
"Woo! Hoo! HOO!" shouts Zee.

The Big Storm carries
Chimp and Zee out of the garden.
Past the dancing trees . . .

higher . . .

and HIGHER . . .

AND **HIGHER!**

Way above Jungletown.

"My goodness! Those little monkeys are heading straight for the sea!" shouts a shopkeeper.

"Help, help, help!" shouts Chimp.
"Put us down!" squeals Zee.

But the Big Storm
will not put them down.
It sweeps them through
the dark sky . . .
closer and closer to
the Very Dangerous Cliffs.

"Chimp and Zee will
be lost at sea," says the
old lighthouse keeper sadly.

Here are Mumkey and Papakey, chasing the flyaway twins.

Faster, faster, faster!

Papakey pedals up the hill. Right to the top
of the Very Dangerous Cliffs. But he is too late!
Chimp and Zee have already gone . . .

high above the wild and wicked waves.

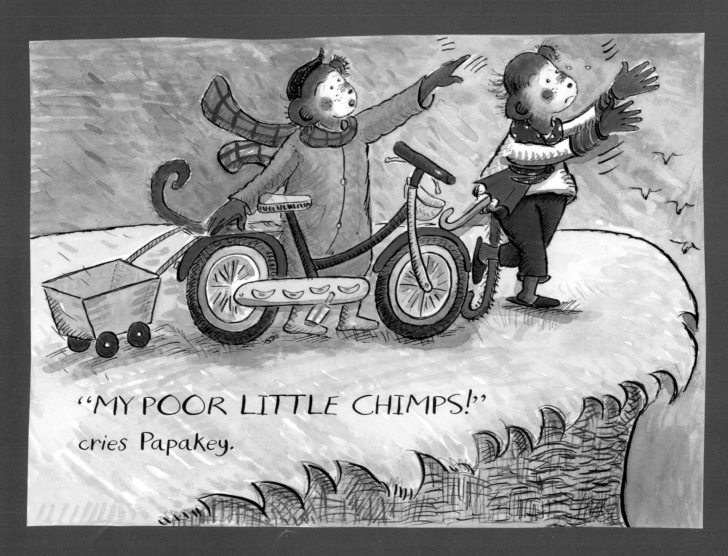

"MY POOR LITTLE CHIMPS!"
cries Papakey.

"O-OO-M!!,"

booms the Big Storm.

Quick as lightning, Mumkey does an amazing thing —
she grabs her umbrella and
climbs high onto Papakey's shoulders.

Mumkey stretches . . .

higher and higher

and HIGHER.

She pulls down her sheet and . . .

her wet and windy Chimp and Zee.

"Chimp did it."

"Zee did it."

"I wasn't even there."

"Zee did it."

"Chimp did it."

"It's just NOT FAIR!"

"Oh, you chumpy chimps!" says Mumkey.

Then Papakey hurries through the flooded fields.

Past the rushing river. Back to their home in the coconut tree.

Quick! Up the ladder!
Slam the door!

"We do not want
the Big Storm in here."

Then Mumkey lights the stove.

Papakey fries hot bananas.

Chimp and Zee cuddle together,

snug as twins in a rug;

and they sing songs together,

all through the wild afternoon . . .

"Families can be stormy sometimes," says Papakey.
"Yes," says Mumkey, "but whatever
the weather, we'll always be together."

Mumkey and Papakey and . . .

Chimp and Zee

as the sun comes out
in the coconut tree.